Mercury

Lori Dittmer

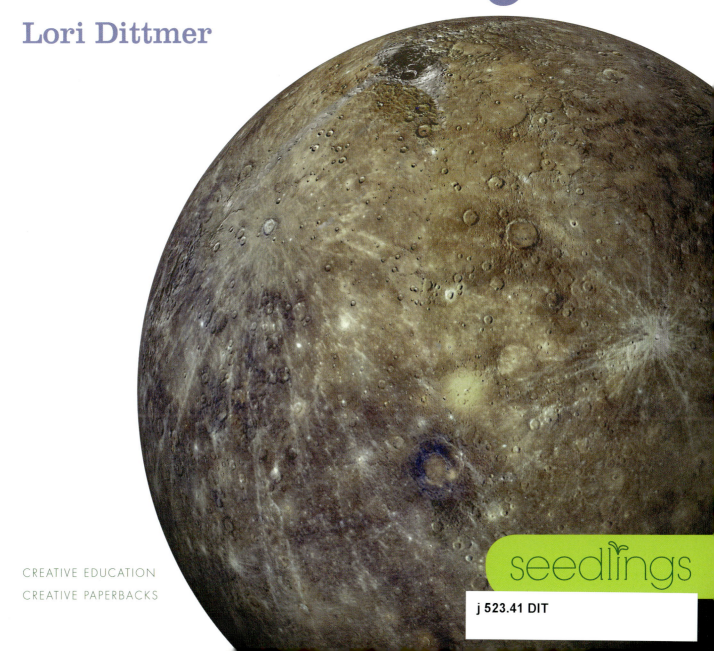

CREATIVE EDUCATION
CREATIVE PAPERBACKS

seedlings

Published by Creative Education and Creative Paperbacks
P.O. Box 227, Mankato, Minnesota 56002
Creative Education and Creative Paperbacks
are imprints of The Creative Company
www.thecreativecompany.us

Design by Ellen Huber; production by Joe Kahnke
Art direction by Rita Marshall
Printed in the United States of America

Photographs by Alamy (Science Photo Library), Corbis (NASA),
Getty Images (MARK GARLICK/SCIENCE PHOTO LIBRARY),
iStockphoto (FlashMyPixel, ikonacolor, m-gucci), Mary Evans
Picture Library (Barry Norman Collection), NASA (Johns Hopkins
University Applied Physics Laboratory/Carnegie Institution of
Washington), Science Source (Richard Bizley, Walter Myers,
Detlev van Ravenswaay), Shutterstock (Pavel Chagochkin, Mopic),
SuperStock (Science Photo Library)

Library of Congress Cataloging-in-Publication Data
Names: Dittmer, Lori, author.
Title: Mercury / Lori Dittmer.
Series: Seedlings.
Includes bibliographical references and index.
Summary: A kindergarten-level introduction to the planet
Mercury, covering its orbital process and such defining
features as its extreme temperatures, craters, and name.
Identifiers: ISBN 987-1-60818-916-8 (hardcover) / ISBN 987-1-
62832-532-4 (pbk) / ISBN 987-1-56660-968-5 (eBook)
This title has been submitted for CIP
processing under LCCN 2017938980.

CCSS: RI.K.1, 2, 3, 4, 5, 6, 7;
RI.1.1, 2, 3, 4, 5, 6, 7; RF.K.1, 3; RF.1.1

First Edition HC 9 8 7 6 5 4 3 2 1
First Edition PBK 9 8 7 6 5 4 3 2 1

TABLE OF CONTENTS

Hello, Mercury!

Mercury is the closest **planet** to the sun.

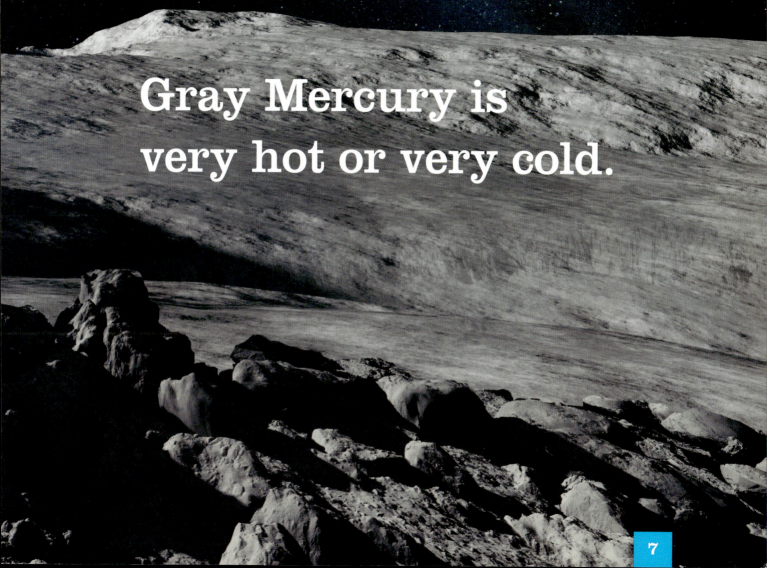

Gray Mercury is
very hot or very cold.

Daytime on Mercury is hot.
It can be 800 °F (427 °C)!

Nights are far below freezing.

Mercury has no moons. The planet is marked with craters. Space rocks hit Mercury a lot.

Small Mercury is fast. It takes just 88 days to orbit the sun.

Astronomers study planets.

They found Mercury thousands of years ago. They named it for an old story about a speedy god. He delivered messages.

Winds from the sun blow across Mercury. Space rocks zoom past.

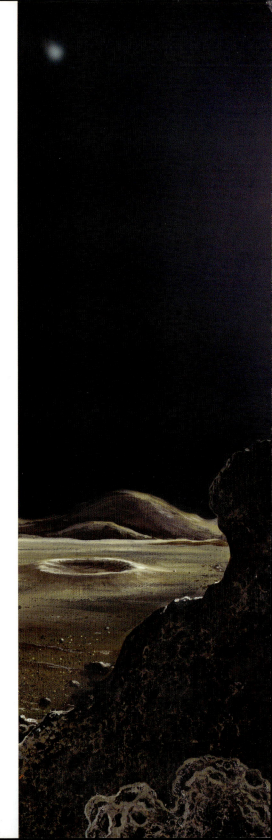

Goodbye, Mercury!

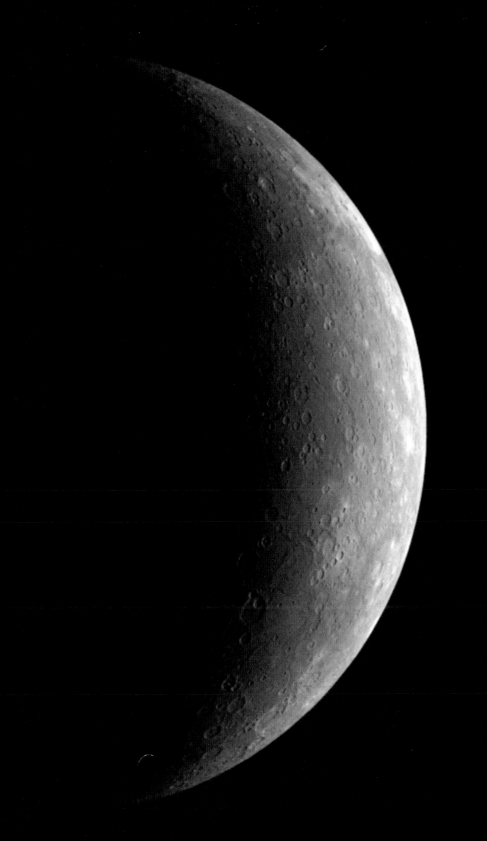

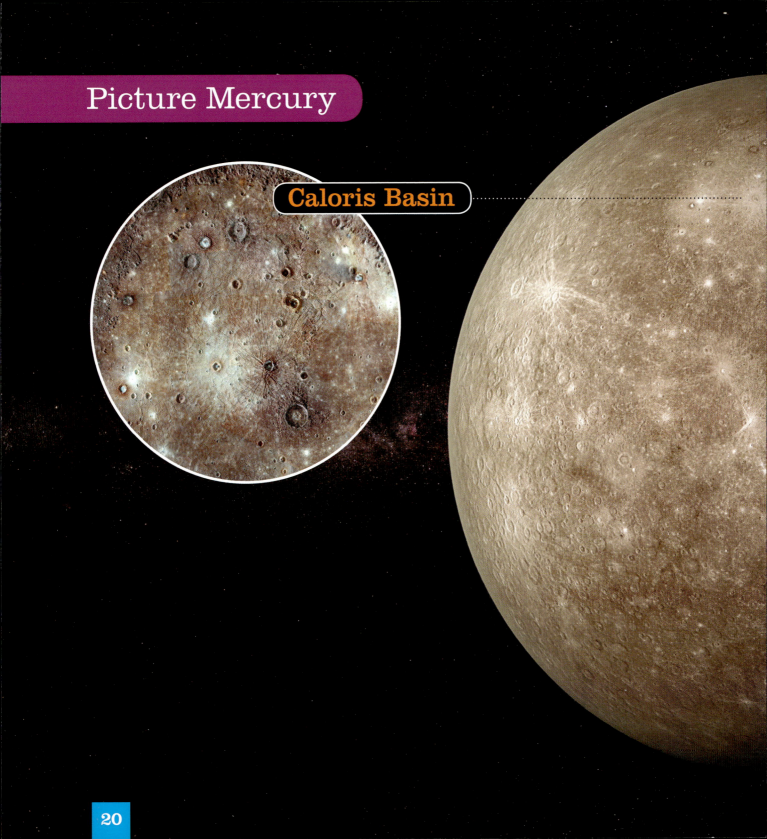

Picture Mercury

Caloris Basin

surface

lava flow

crater

Words to Know

craters: bowl-shaped dents in the ground

god: a being thought to have special powers and control over the world

orbit: the path a planet, moon, or other object takes around something else in outer space

planet: a rounded object that moves around a star

Read More

Adamson, Thomas K. *Do You Really Want to Visit Mercury?* Mankato, Minn.: Amicus, 2014.

Loewen, Nancy. *Nearest to the Sun: The Planet Mercury.* Minneapolis: Picture Window Books, 2008.

Websites

NASA Jet Propulsion Laboratory: Kids
http://www.jpl.nasa.gov/kids/
Build a spacecraft or play a planetary game.

National Geographic Kids: Mission to Mercury
http://kids.nationalgeographic.com/explore/space/mission
-to-mercury/#mercury-planet.jpg
Learn how Mercury moves through the solar system.

Index